Grandma's Hurrying Child

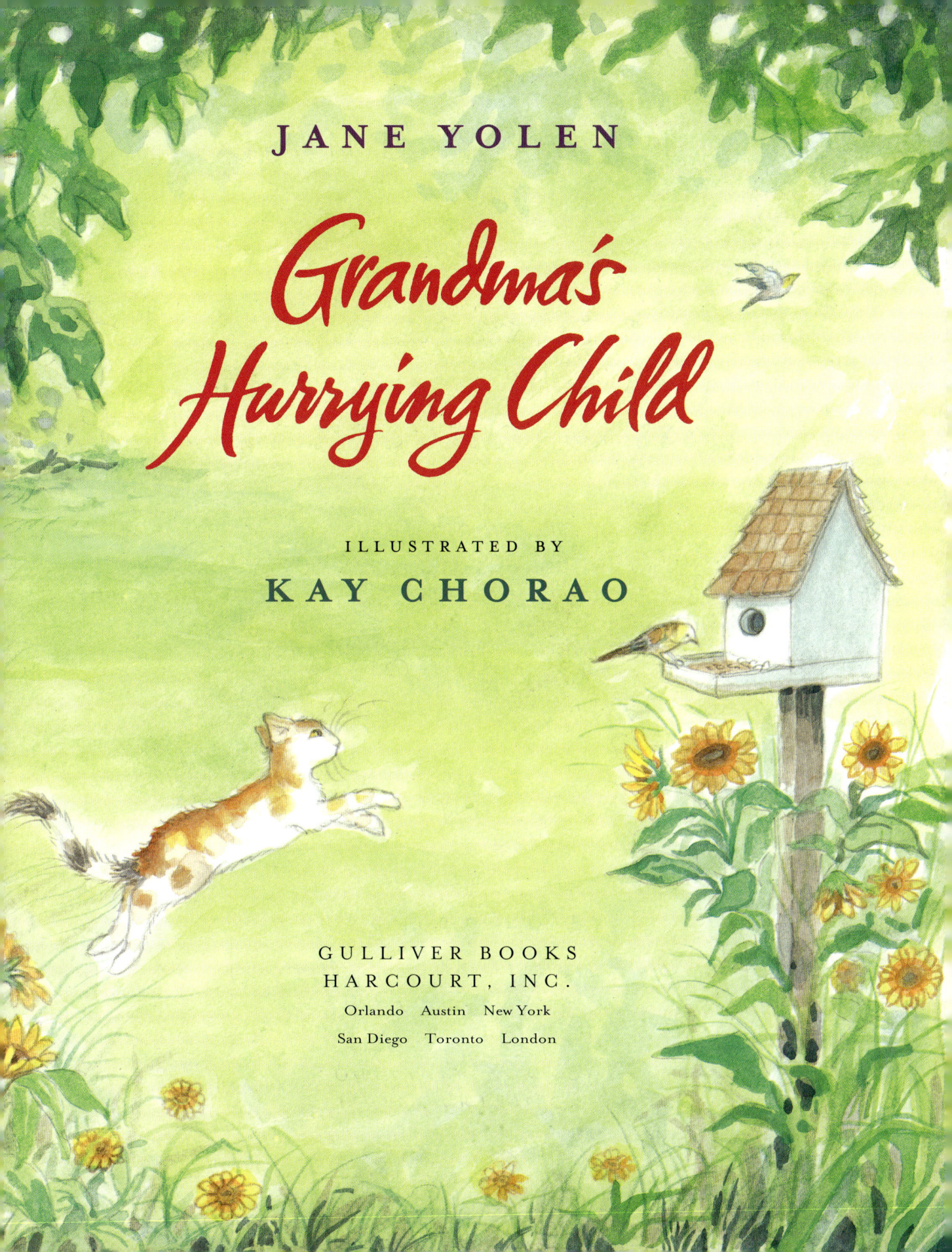

JANE YOLEN

Grandma's Hurrying Child

ILLUSTRATED BY
KAY CHORAO

GULLIVER BOOKS
HARCOURT, INC.
Orlando Austin New York
San Diego Toronto London

Text copyright © 2005 by Jane Yolen
Illustrations copyright © 2005 by Kay Sproat Chorao

All rights reserved. No part of this publication may be reproduced or transmitted
in any form or by any means, electronic or mechanical, including photocopy, recording, or any
information storage and retrieval system, without permission in writing from the publisher.

Requests for permission to make copies of any part of the work should be mailed to the following address:
Permissions Department, Harcourt, Inc., 6277 Sea Harbor Drive, Orlando, Florida 32887-6777.

www.HarcourtBooks.com

Gulliver Books is a trademark of Harcourt, Inc.,
registered in the United States of America and/or other jurisdictions.

Library of Congress Cataloging-in-Publication Data
Yolen, Jane.
Grandma's hurrying child/Jane Yolen; illustrated by Kay Chorao.
p. cm.
"Gulliver Books."
Summary: Grandma tells her grandchild the story of the child's birth
and how they both hurried to make it there on time.
[1. Babies—Fiction. 2. Birth—Fiction. 3. Grandmothers—Fiction.] I. Chorao, Kay, ill. II. Title.
PZ7.Y78Gp 2005
[E]—dc22   2003027256
ISBN 0-15-201813-1

First edition

A C E G H F D B

The illustrations in this book were created in watercolor,
gouache, and colored pencil on 4-ply hot press watercolor paper.
The title was hand lettered by Georgia Deaver.
The text type was set in Mrs. Eaves.
Color separations by Bright Arts Ltd., Hong Kong
Printed and bound by Tien Wah Press, Singapore
This book was printed on totally chlorine-free Stora Enso Matte paper.
Production supervision by Pascha Gerlinger
Designed by Linda Lockowitz

For Maddison Jane, because I wrote this right after you were born
—J. Y.

For Ian and Sylvia, who presented two grandmas with a beloved hurrying child
—K. S. C.

"TELL ME, tell me again, Grandma," Maddy said.
"Tell me about the day I was born.
Tell me how I was a hurrying child.
And how you hurried across three states to meet me."

Grandma smiled and put down her knitting.
"Ten days before you were due," she said,
"your mama stood up and put her hands on her belly.
'Oh my!' Mama said, because she could feel you inside,
eager to be born.

Your papa jumped up and called me on the phone.
'Hurry, Grandma, hurry,' he cried,
because I lived so far away.
Then he grabbed the little case by the front door.
His face was like chalk on a smudged board.

Your mama bent over the waiting cradle.
'Be ready,' she whispered, 'for my dark-haired girl.'
Papa hovered in the door. 'Hurry, hurry,' he said.
Mama smiled. 'Do not worry.
This is not a hurrying child.'

But far away in my own little house,
I worried I would not get there in time.

Mama straightened up suddenly.

'Oh my—I think she's ready.'

Papa said, 'This child who is not a hurrying child?'

'I have changed my mind,' said Mama.

'She is in a *big* hurry now.'

Far away I hurried, too.

They went outside to the car
and Papa opened the door, *snick-snack*.
He helped Mama in, then *snick-snack* closed the door.

I got on the train. *Clickety-clack*, went the wheels.
Snick-snack, clickety-clack.
Everybody hurried.

At the hospital, a nurse helped Mama into a high bed.
'Do not worry,' said the nurse, but she ran to call the doctor.

And on the train that went *clickety-clack,*
with my knitting needles going *snickety-snack,*
I wished the train could go faster.

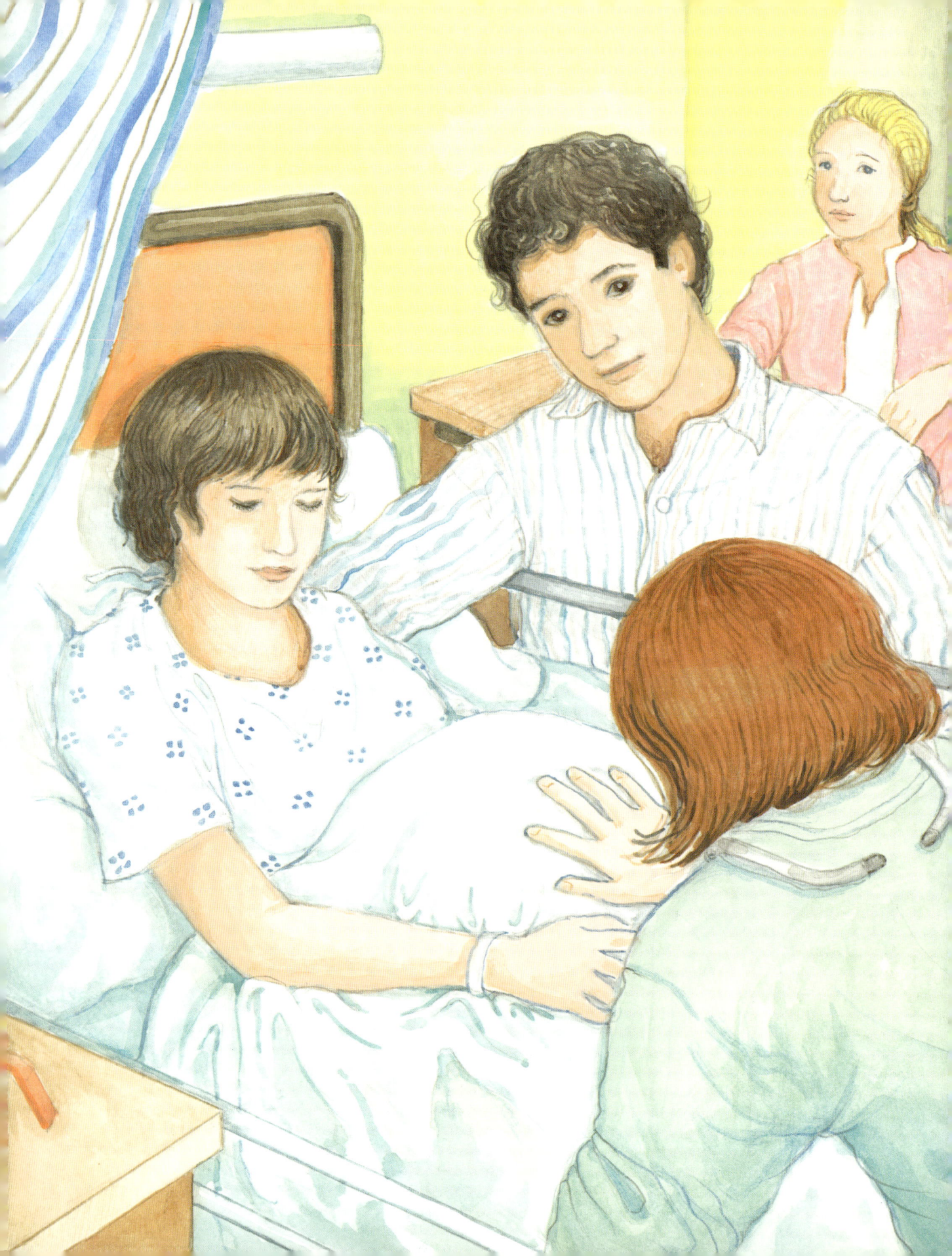

The doctor came with long strides and put her hand on Mama's belly. The doctor's eyebrows shot up. She nodded at the nurse.
'*This* is a hurrying child,' she said.

While Mama pushed and breathed hard,
and made sounds like my train
coming into the station,
I hurried with my traveling bag off the train
and out into the street.

Papa held Mama's hand.
He said, 'Grandma is hurrying here, hurrying as fast as she can.'"

"And I was hurrying, too!" added Maddy.

"In the hospital, Papa stopped saying anything else but counting:
One,
    two,
        three,
            four . . .

and out you came in a great *big* hurry,
your head crowned with dark hair,
your blue-sky eyes opened wide.
And you were crying, 'I am here! I am here!'
Mama held out her arms saying,
'My hurrying child! My hurrying child!'

Just then, in I came all out of breath
from running up the hospital steps,
and saw you, your face still bright red
from all that hurrying.
I wrapped you in the blanket I had knit
and kissed you on your dark hair.

Then we smiled at one another,
because we knew then
what you had known all along,
that you were, indeed,
Grandma's hurrying child."